I0624106

The Unclean
Nuzo Onoh

Canaan-Star Publishing

First published by Canaan-Star Publishing, United Kingdom in (2014)
www.canaan-star.co.uk

Aurelia Leo Publishers – Dominion (2020)
This edition (2020)

ISBN: 978-1-909484-37-5

This story is dedicated to my beautiful mother, the late Caroline Onoh, the consummate story-teller and survivor.

...And my sister, Ambassador Lilian Onoh, the original "Gono"

About The Author

Nuzo Onoh is a Nigerian-British writer and pioneer of African horror. Born in Enugu, in the Eastern part of Nigeria (formerly known as Biafra), she lived through the civil war between Biafra and Nigeria (1967 – 1970), an experience that left a strong impact on her and continues to influence her writing to date.

She attended Queen's school, Enugu, Nigeria, before proceeding to the Quaker boarding school, The Mount School, York, (England) and finally, St Andrew's Tutorial college, Cambridge, (England) from where she obtained her A' levels. Nuzo holds both a Law degree and a Masters degree in Writing from Warwick University, (England).

Her writing has featured in multiple anthologies and she continues to be on the forefront of pioneering the regional horror genre, African Horror. She has two daughters, Candice and Jija, and lives in The United Kingdom with her cat, Tinkerbell.

Praise for

The Unclean

"Well written, evocative, historical, tragic… it's a rich story – rich in evoking the setting, the culture, the entwined and confusing aspects of religions and beliefs, superstitions and societal pressure and supplications placed on women and individuals who are different…"

(*Cosmic Roots and Eldritch Shores*)

"Dark, intense, gruesome, not at all pleasant, and masterfully put together".

(SFF Reviews)

"The Unclean" by Nuzo Onoh was for me an extraordinary discovery…the story grabbed me and didn't let me go. It filled me with emotions--sadness, anger, grief and hope."

(*The Middle Shelf Science-fiction and Fantasy Books Reviews Blog*)

"The Unclean: Beautifully tragic opening"

(Hellnotes)

"The Unclean" by Nuzo Onoh is a grim story ...there's a heavy supernatural element, but it's the slow build to the unsettling finish that gives the quiet thrill. Powerful writing here.

(Nerine Dorman blogspot)

"The Unclean ... was challenging and disturbing, staying with me long after I had finished the book." *(The British Fantasy Society)*

"The Unclean...this story by itself, bereft of any supernatural elements, caused me to shed tears." *(Lovecraft Ezine)*

"superb and harrowing...It is extremely powerful."

(Featured Futures)

The Unclean

"There is nothing the eyes will see that will cause them to shed blood-tears"

– Igbo Proverb

The Unclean

Chapter One

(Ukari Forest - 9pm)

My husband's corpse lies on the raffia mat, spread underneath the giant Iroko tree that towers over the thick vegetation of Ukari Forest. The Iroko tree is legendary in the ten clans of Ukari and even beyond. Its broad branches reach up to the skies, fighting for airspace with the eagles and the kites. Its circumference covers at least eight arms-length of marriage-age men. The other trees in the forest bow their leafy obeisance to the Iroko tree, paying homage to their great lord, just as the humans of Ukari village kneel to it.

All is still. Nothing breaks the grave-like silence of the vast forest. Apart from the occasional snake or lizard, no other creature stirs in the perennial gloom of this accursed forest. From my kneeling position by my late husband's body, I force my bloodied eyes to look upon his reviled face, coal-dusted by death and decay. His features, swarthy and harsh, have not yielded their cruelty to death. The white cloth shrouding his bloated body is stained with the death fluids seeping from his fast decomposing body.

In the two nights I've spent in the forest with my husband's corpse, I have been unable to keep my eyes from his face....and IT. I feel its malignancy, the threat in its unnatural turgidity. I live in terror of what IT would do to me should I take my gaze away from its terrible erectness.

I look away, return my gaze to his face. My body shudders yet again, expecting those swollen lids to lift, his cold eyes promising harsh retribution for sins I can never recollect. Yet, I cannot escape. I am rooted to my husband's side by limb-freezing terror. My heart leaps into my mouth, filling it with bile and panic each time the trees stir, the dry leaves rustle or an owl hoots his midnight vigil from a distant tree. Had I slept, my dreams would have been dreams of escape, freedom - and peace. But I am forbidden that relief, chained as I am to my husband's corpse by the witch-doctors' powerful incantations and the customs of our land.

I am a prisoner in a jail without bars. I am the condemned, convicted before her trial. I am the accused, facing her judgement at the one-man jury in the court of the great Iroko tree, known to the villagers as The Tree of Truth. The Tree of Truth is the final arbiter in every dispute in the village, the righteous judge and jury that condemns and sentences with ruthless efficiency. It is said that none who is guilty ever escapes its merciless justice. Its roots are swollen with the blood and cries of its victims, men, women and even children, accused of crimes ranging from witchcraft to night-flying. And I, Desdemona, first daughter of Ukah, wife of Agu of Onori Clan, have joined that wretched fraternity of The Tree. I am a condemned criminal awaiting my fate beneath the unforgiving leaves of The Tree of Truth.

As I prepare to endure my third and final night by the side of the putrid body of my late husband, I know with a feeling of total despair that my ordeal is far from over. Even if by some unbelievable stroke of fortune The Tree of Truth rejects my blood; if by some divine intervention my husband's vengeful spirit fails to strike me dead by dawn as is widely expected in our village, I could yet be dispatched to my own ancestors' hell by a myriad of foes, too strong, too powerful, for a mere widow to resist.

For, I am the most accursed of widows. I am a widow without offspring, cursed with the womb of a man, my belly filled with soured eggs that will never again yield the precious fruit of a child. Even worse, I am a widow without a son, left without protection like a day-old baby abandoned in the middle of an African thunderstorm, exposed to the flings and thumps of the merciless force of nature. No one will speak or fight for me, neither in the human, ancestral or spiritual realms.

For my failure to provide my husband with an heir and name-protector; for my desperate and foolish attempts to produce that precious gift; for my own mad folly and ignorance, I will pay with my life when the cock crows in the dawn and his relatives come to extract the life from beneath my chest - my coward's heart, my foolish heart.

Chapter Two

I married Agu a few months after I turned seventeen, just one year past the age of female wisdom. It was a time of great changes in our country, a time when people said the white men would give us back our land and return to their own. The calendar in our parlour had the year, 1953, stamped on it. It also had pictures of our new ruler, Queen Elizabeth 11, on all its twelve pages. There used to be pictures of the king. But the king was dead and the queen now owned our lands and calendars.

Agu arrived at our house one rainy day as we made to prepare Papa's lunch of *yam fufu* and bush-meat soup. I was in the smoke-clouded kitchen, attempting to keep the kerosene stove going, when the kitchen door flew open and my little brother, Ibe, rushed in, all excitement and glee, knocking over Mama's wooden stool in his haste.

'Desee, Papa wants you now,' his eyes were wide with what seemed like awe, his voice pitched like a girl's. I wondered what had given the sudden animation to his customary indolent disposition. Ibe took his role as the only son very seriously. And both Papa and Mama made sure we, the daughters, recognised and respected his privileged status as "heir," regardless of our superiority in both age and intellect. I had already passed out of senior school with grades that were good enough to secure me a teaching apprenticeship at the village primary school. My sister, Gono, also seemed certain to follow in my footsteps.

But Ibe, despite the attention and praise lavished on him by our parents and family at large, never succeeded in producing a report card that could make any teacher or parent proud. Yet, Papa would insist on giving him the chair of honour in the family living room, right next to grandfather's stone grave, while Mama would chant her "hero song" whenever he sneezed, coughed or even farted, her face glowing with a mixture of pride, determination and a sad kind of martyrdom that left one wondering why she'd even bothered giving birth to her precious son in the first place.

> *"Jealous people, leave my tiger alone;*
> *Envious people, look at my prize;*
> *Evil people, turn your eyes from my son,*
> *my hero, my solace, my king."*

And well might she praise the little sod, since without his timely appearance, Papa would have replaced her with a second wife to produce the much-wanted heir and "name-protector." As Papa was fond of telling my sister and me, a woman has no name, no religion, no country, no custom and no honour except that given her by a man, a husband. Ibe's name said it all - clansmen, brothers!

Ibe was the only one amongst us given an Igbo name, showing how valued he was. We, the girls, had been left to the mercy of poor Mama when it came time for name selection. She in turn had turned to her "learned" brother, Uncle Silas, who had promptly lumbered us with the most highfalutin names imaginable, courtesy of one Mr Shakespeare of England. Everyone knew me as Day-see-mona (Desee, for short), except my schoolteachers, who had struggled in my student years to read out *Desdemona* in the class register every morning. My younger sister was known as Gono to everyone, but diligently wrote her full name in her textbooks - *Goneril.*

'Desee, hurry up or Papa will get angry with you,' Ibe was almost hopping by the open kitchen door. I heard a grunt and turned to look at Gono, who had stopped pounding the *yam fufu* in the wooden mortar as soon as Ibe made his announcement. Her brows dipped in a frown of displeasure. I was unsure who her anger was directed against - Ibe or Papa, both of whom she loathed with equal intensity.

'What does he want with Desee?' Gono barked at Ibe. 'Can't he see we're busy preparing lunch for you two bigheads?' She shot Ibe a look that dripped with contempt, her body, wiry and small, as tense as a featherweight boxer's in a boxing ring. Aggression emitted from every pore in her body as she stood clutching the long wooden pestle. She looked as if she intended to bash in someone's head with it.

Ibe looked at her and quickly averted his eyes. 'I don't know,' he mumbled, slinking out of the kitchen, but not before I caught a shifty look in his eyes that convinced me he was lying - as usual. That boy would lie to God Himself if he ever made it to St Peter's gates. Gono was the only one amongst us - Papa included - who inspired some form of fear in the lout.

The Unclean

Gono's temper was notorious in the five clans and many had already predicted she would remain a spinster with her harridan's temperament - a fact that pleased rather than dismayed her. Even Papa avoided sending her on errands, at least, as much as he could without appearing weak. Gono was the only one of his children that never cried when he took the birch to her.

I entered the sitting room, hard on Ibe's heels, to see two strangers, both men, seated on the whitewashed wooden benches that circled our sitting room. Each of the strangers, including Papa, cradled a ceramic mug of palm-wine in their hands, while a brimming cup of the brew was placed atop my grandfather's raised grave positioned in the centre of the parlour. Papa never drank palm wine without offering some to my grandfather. I did a small curtesy to the seated strangers and a deeper one to my grandfather's grave.

'Aahh! Desee, come sit down my daughter,' Papa patted the chair of honour, the seat next to his own and nearest to the elevated rectangular grave, Ibe's special chair! Papa's face beamed with a benevolence I'd only ever witnessed when he addressed Ibe. More worryingly, he had called me Desee, instead of his habitual "*Agbogho*" - girl. Something was clearly wrong. My heart was thudding as I took the proffered seat, ignoring Ibe's displeased frown as he settled for the little stool by the snuff table.

'These gentlemen are from Ukari,' Papa said, with a nod at the strangers. I glanced up quickly and lowered my eyelids just as rapidly, to preserve my modesty. 'They've come a long way indeed to see us, or should I say, to see you, my daughter.' Papa chuckled in a manner that could have been interpreted as coy had he been a woman. I wanted to hide my face beneath the thin fabric of my yellow cotton dress; such was my discomfiture.

'Yes indeed. We have travelled a six-hour journey to come and view your famed beauty,' I heard one of the men say, the old grey one. The oily quality to his voice repelled me. I felt the heat of embarrassment on my face, at the same time feeling a sudden prick of apprehension at the back of my neck.

'Our son here is Agu, son of Onori of the Onori clan,' the old man continued. His hair was sprinkled with ash, as were his bushy brows and thick beard, giving him the look of a grey-dappled hyena. But despite the whites in his hair, I could tell he wasn't an old man, merely prematurely grey, as happens on occasion with certain reincarnations.

I felt my soul reject his at first sight, a clear sign we had been antagonists in a previous incarnation. Something in his ferocious gaze wilted my spirit and I kept my eyes downcast.

'Agu is a prosperous trader and travels as far as *Ugwu-Hausa*, the Muslim northern territories, to buy and sell various foodstuff,' continued Grey-Hyena, nodding at the young man next to him. 'In fact, Agu owns the only storey building in our village and a Mercedes Benz, which you can see parked outside your father's compound,' his voice was oiled with pride.

Instinctively, I glanced out of the open curtainless window, as did Ibe, to see a white car - a large silver-wheeled car - getting washed by the pouring rain outside our compound. Papa feigned disinterest though I could read a gleam in his eyes that indicated otherwise to me. But he was a proud man and I guess he deserved his dignity. A bicycle, even an almost new British Raleigh that had cost him a handsome sum, could never compete with a Benz.

'As we were telling your good father before you came in, we'd heard of the famed beauty of the white chicken he housed beneath his roof. So, we decided to rush in and express our interest in purchasing that white chicken before others, less worthy, beat us to the market.' The grey one smiled at me, a front tooth missing.

The Unclean

I quickly averted my gaze and glued my eyes to my hands, which had suddenly started trembling as if I'd been struck down with malaria.

'Your father has been very kind in indicating his willingness to sell us his precious chicken. So, we thought it was a good time for you to meet your future husband, Agu, before we begin formal negotiations for the marriage rites. After all, a girl must be allowed some choice in these matters even though the ultimate decision rests with her esteemed father - and rightly so,' Grey-Hyena gave a small chuckle, which was echoed by Papa and even the little idiot, Ibe.

I felt the racing of my heart. *Some choice indeed!* It was as I had feared. Papa was marrying me off to a complete stranger, a man whose name or face I have neither heard nor seen till this very day; and just as I was about to complete my apprenticeship and progress to full teacher status. I felt the sting of tears in my eyes as my palms broke out in hot sweat. I wanted to get up and run out of that crowded room with the stuffy odour of strange bodies and palm-wine.

But fear of Papa's wrath and a cramp of embarrassment kept me glued onto Ibe's special seat. I forced my eyes up and took my first proper look at my future husband, Agu.

What I saw was a man, short of stature and lacking in bulk. Age-wise, he was at the peak of his manhood, somewhere between thirty and forty years. It was difficult to tell his exact age because of his small size. He was dressed in an *Agbada*, a loose native garb covered in an assortment of animal prints. His hair was trimmed close to his skull, giving him an almost bald look. Sat next to his older relative on our wooden bench, his head barely reached Grey-Hyena's shoulders.

Yet, there was a carriage to his head, an arrogance of bearing that marked him as the leader despite his puny size. He was dark, very black-skinned, like the

Enugu coal miners at the end of their work shift beneath the bowels of the earth. His eyes were small, closely set. There was an expression in them that reminded me of the eyes of the frozen fish heads we used in cooking Papa's chilli pepper-soup. Their black depths betrayed little emotion as they settled on my person; just the detached assessment of a trader inspecting some ware before making final purchase. Even when he smiled at me as our eyes briefly met for the first time, there was no gentling in his pupils or his lips – thin, fleshless lips – unusual in a native of our country. Something about him frightened me, placed a cold hand over my heart, a silent terror that didn't subside even after I got up and noticed how I towered over him by at least three fingers' length.

Instinctively, I hunched my shoulders, feeling ashamed of my tall slenderness, emphasised into giant proportions by his small stature. I caught the strangers' nod of satisfaction as I returned to Papa's side and knew with a tight feeling in my stomach that my fate was sealed.

Despite knowing - always having known - that my duty as a daughter was to reward Papa's sacrifices with a good bride price, it still rankled that I was denied the choice of deciding who should pay the price on my head. I had secretly hoped it would be Chudi, one of the teachers in the primary school where I did my apprenticeship – tall, handsome and intelligent Chudi, with the gentle smile and soft voice of a deep thinker. Instead, Papa had effectively sold me to the illiterate trader with the cold eyes and thin lips. I did not doubt that I would fetch a handsome bride price as a result of my light skin and secondary school education. I was after all, the reincarnation of my great-grandmother, who had been famed in her lifetime for her amazing fairness and beauty. The children she reincarnated in within the family, including Mama, had a special black circle on their stomachs. All except me.

The Unclean

Instead, I had something more visible than that special birthmark. I had great-grandmother's hair; hair so long and fine that people often wondered if there was a secret white ancestry somewhere in our bloodline. Others, with malicious blood in their veins, would say I was lucky to have escaped being an albino, those unfortunate people in our community, cursed with skin that must forever hide from the sun.

I went through my days more concerned with my books and my ambition for a successful teaching career than my purported beauty. My command of the spoken English language was second to none in the entire village and people would often ask me to draft or read letters for them, a fact that pleased Papa no end.

When in a good mood, he would call me "*Onye-nkuzi*" – teacher, with a teasing gleam in his eyes, secretly proud of my achievement and literary prowess. Otherwise, on most days, especially when my brother Ibe had performed particularly badly in his exams,

Papa would berate me for the precious time I wasted with my incessant reading, reminding me of the reason for my education.

'I don't want you to forget that I only allowed you an education to ensure you command a good bride price and hopefully, marry one of the new lawyers or doctors that are on the lookout for educated wives. Keep that in mind and don't go wasting your time with those useless books.'

My sister, Gono, on the other hand, with skin as dark as our father's, even if smoother to the touch and glossier to the sight, was not burdened with any such great expectations. I once heard one of our elderly aunties say that Gono's beauty would outlast my own because she wasn't a morning flower like me, the light-skinned daughter. She wouldn't bloom early and fade away early like I would. Hers was the enduring beauty that would weather the caprices of time and the cruelty of man.

The Unclean

I don't think Papa or Gono bought into her theory. Papa said that Gono's only hope of bagging a respectable bride price lay in acquiring an exceptional education, but only if her stubbornness allowed her to complete secondary school without getting expelled. But we knew we would be lucky if Gono deigned to give any man her hand in marriage for a bride price, respectable or otherwise. I pitied my sister because I feared she might never know the joys of marriage, as was the right of every woman as nature intended, a situation I suddenly found myself now facing without any feeling of joy.

Later that night, after our guests had gone, I cried as I had never cried in my seventeen years of growing up in Iburu village. I cried for the impending loss of my home, my family, my freedom, my career, my burgeoning affection for my fellow apprentice teacher, Chudi. In particular, I cried for the man, Agu, that cold stranger with the icy eyes and thin lips, who was soon to become my husband and my master. And I wondered in silent despair, if my life would ever be the same again.

Chapter Three

(Ukari Forest – 11.45pm)

The cold night wears on in the dreadful forest, as I feel the bile rise in my mouth for the umpteenth time. I turn away from my husband's corpse and retch into the wet grass, already stinking with my urine and vomit. The pain in my stomach is unbearable. It feels as if the imps of Satan have taken residence in my belly, wrenching my innards for their sport. The thirst burns my throat and my body shivers and trembles with cold and hunger. I cast my eyes, made blurry by tears and bruises, at the water jug that stands on the mat next to my husband's body. I stretch out a trembling hand in its direction. Then I stop, pull back my hand as if stung by a scorpion, as remembrance floods my memory, dulled by four days of starvation and sleep deprivation.

The Unclean

The water in the jug is corpse water, the water used in bathing the decomposing body of my husband; the water I had been forced to drink in the presence of all the clan as punishment for my crime. In the aftermath of Agu's death, I was held down by cruel hands, my nose squeezed shut, as endless cups of corpse water were forced into my open mouth in relentless succession.

I cannot begin to describe the taste of that hideous fluid, the sour salty tang, the cloying milkiness of pus, the lingering bitterness of decayed flesh. The more I retched the more I was fed the cloudy corpse water, with punches, slaps and curses to compound my humiliation. And now, even as I crouch beside my late husband's corpse, I can still feel the swelling on my face from the beatings. My ears still ring with the invectives heaped on them – Murderer! Husband killer! Child murderer! Mermaid witch! Evil stranger! Wicked sorceress! Ogbanje! Man-woman!

And much more… much worse. And all because of my desperation, my bad Chi *my foolishness, a desperate need that has now brought me to this wretched state.*

As I listen to the painful growling of my stomach, I draw in my knees to keep within the salt-lined boundary set by the three witchdoctors on the hard soil of the forest, and turn my eyes to the dry-barked trunk of The Tree of Truth. The tree hulks over us, its branches stretching into black infinity. Its massive trunk is scarred with ridges of dry gum, flaky barks and aborted stumps of unborn branches…and blood; a red-wash of blood. There is an ancient power within its unfathomable depths that shrouds it with wisdom and terror. Within its all-knowing roots lies my salvation.

I bare my body and my soul to the towering guardian of justice. I plead for its vindication, its protection, its forgiveness. And when finally my wailing voice grows hoarse, whimpers into a whisper, I bury my head in my hands as I allow my mind to travel back into the terrible events that have led to my present sorry predicament and could yet lead to my ultimate demise.

Chapter Four

From the day I entered Agu's house as his bride, I ceased expecting anything good. I had always believed that I was amongst the fortunate people born with a good *Chi*, favoured by good fortune and my ancestors, due to my good deeds in my previous life. Even my Igbo name, Chioma, good personal god, reinforced my belief.

My marriage shattered that conception.

As the weeks merged into months and the swollen moon brought in numerous years, I gradually became immune to the bad things that befell me in my matrimonial hell. Queen Ill-fortune sent her minions to me with the regularity of mosquito bites – broken glasses, stolen wrappers off the wash-line, burnt Egusi soup pots, punches from my husband and his three fat sisters, a crushed finger from the grinding stone. They were all small and regular irritants, harmless like most mosquito bites but malaria-deadly when the big one struck – Queen Ill-fortune herself, the all-powerful and all-knowing ruler of my destiny, the controller of my bad *Chi*.

She visited me with the regularity of my monthly curse, usually on the last day of the full moon, when the hidden madness in men's souls are raised from their dormant sleep to wreak violence and evil on womankind. Queen Ill-fortune's visits always left my soul as bloodied as the woman's curse that plagued my soured groin.

As I observed the birth of each new moon, my heart felt like a bare bottom sat on a heaving ant-hill. My eyes would seek out its thin curves as I pounded my husband's *Akpu* cassava meal in the hollow of my wooden mortar. Every sundown, as I brought in the washing from the lines or ushered in the goats into their pen, I would feel the slow terror build in my heart as the moon began to swell, fed on its diet of rain and clouds….and malice.

Soon, it would be a perfect melon of doom, ready to burst its calamity on my braided head. Queen Ill-fortune rides the full moon as every child and adult knows. Together, they invoke evil, awake the dead and spread devastation along their route, as they journey through mankind's lands and lives. Everyone cursed with a bad *Chi* knows to dread the arrival of the full moon.

Initially, I was blissfully ignorant of the unholy union of these two deities, a malevolent partnership that brought nothing but misery to my life in my matrimonial home. I started keeping score after the loss of my sanity on that accursed day, the eve of the New Yam festival.

***

Married life had never been a life of songs and dances for me because I was a learned wife from a different village. I quickly learned that there can be no pleasing mankind when feelings of inferiority plague the souls of humanity. Nothing I did was ever approved or appreciated by my in-laws and the villagers. I could have turned water into wine for them like our Lord Jesus did and they would have still found me wanting. I did not go out of my way to prove my intellectual superiority to them, but their knowledge of my superior education doomed every goodwill I could have hoped to receive from them.

Things took a turn for the worse when four years went by and I failed to produce the desired heir for my husband. Worse, I was blessed neither with a miscarriage or a stillbirth. Despite Father O'Keefe's novenas on my behalf, nothing stirred in my womb. It remained as fruitless as a man's stomach.

One day, Agu's eldest and fattest sister, Uzo, took matters into her hands and dragged me to their witchdoctor to find a solution to my barrenness. We arrived at the thatch-roofed mud house of the witchdoctor before the cock crow and waited our turn outside the small compound populated by other troubled souls. The sun was on high-noon by the time we were ushered into the feather-littered shrine of the witchdoctor by a small skewed-eyed boy, bare of feet and dressed in torn undersized trousers.

The man was seated crossed-legged on a hard, cement floor with strange drawings and herbs strewn around him. Blood still dripped from the neck of a freshly butchered chicken hung above the witchdoctor's head. The red fluid soaked his unshaven head, crawling around his face and neck like bloated worms. The sight caused my empty gut to heave. It clawed at my pounding heart till I felt it would burst. I forced my eyes to study the thin veins on my folded hands instead. I felt his eyes on me, burning, probing. My shoulders folded in, rolled forward in a hunched pose of shame, and my hands began to tremble. *What sinful thoughts would he read in my mind? Holy Mary! Please help me! What will he read in my future?*

Suddenly, the decrepit man-demon screamed, pointing a gnarled finger in my direction.

'*Ogbanje!* Water sorceress! Be gone!' he shrieked. Turning glaring eyes at my sister-in-law, he shouted, 'Why have you brought me this accursed daughter of the river Niger?' Still pointing that filthy forefinger at me, his thin arm weighted by multiple charmed amulets, he demanded, 'Why do you bring upon my old head the wrath of the powerful mermaid? Go! Take her away! No one can help her. She belongs to the water, to *Mamiwata*. She's not your brother's wife. She's no mortal man's wife. Her womb will never yield fruit to your brother. Go! Depart from my presence and never return! Go!'

We scurried away, my heart pounding in terror. My sister-in-law abandoned me at the dust road, leaving me to make my own way back to the house. I dreaded what awaited me at Agu's house when he discovered my curse. My mind was like a cauldron of plagued words, bubbling in a stew of insanity and terror – *I am an Ogbanje… a cursed spawn of the evil mermaid and I never even knew! Holy Mary save my soul!*

I wandered the dusty paths, the bushes, even the asphalted main road, thinking, wringing my hands, tugging my braided hair, walking - just walking - with no destination in mind…anything to delay my return to Agu's house.

Within hours of Uzo's return, the entire village had heard of my stigma and my shame. As I made my way back to Agu's compound, people gathered in groups, staring at me, pointing at me, laughing, cursing, spitting as I walked by, my head lowered into my chest. My throat hurt from the salty water I fought to keep behind my eyes. I lost my erect tallness, made suddenly clumsy by the jellying of my legs.

'We should have known she's an *Ogbanje* mermaid,' the fat sisters snapped out the demon over their heads with outstretched arms as I walked past them. 'Have you ever seen anyone so light-skinned unless they're albinos? Or with hair so long it stretches like a mermaid's? But this one is clearly not albino, just water-bleached by her real mother, the evil *Mamiwata* mermaid. Agu should have listened to us when we warned him of the perils of marrying an outsider. One can never tell the curses that follow such people. Oh! Our poor brother!'

By the time Agu returned to the house, a great crowd of relatives had gathered inside his parlour, waiting to fill his ears with the news of my curse. Even before I heard the great roar of his rage rumble past the stairs and into my bedroom, I knew my fate was sealed. With a pounding heart and quaking limbs, I prepared myself to be sent back to my village in shame, a reject of both husband and God.

The Unclean

I was standing by my bed when Agu crashed into my room, the whites of his eyes red-streaked, his pupils as coal, burning with a hate that had hitherto been absent in the four years of our marriage. I barely had the time to mutter the obligatory *"onye-ishi"*, master, when he grabbed my hair, forcing my knees to the floor and dragging me into his room with a strength that defied his puny size and my considerable height.

Once inside his room, he descended on my body with every arsenal at his disposal, venting his fury with his fists, his belt, his birch whips, his walking stick and even the twisted metal clothes-hanger that harboured his array of clothing. My screams fell on deaf consciences. Everyone in that over-populated household heard my howls of pain but no one dared or even wanted to venture into the master's bedroom to halt my thrashing.

I pled for mercy, seeking his forgiveness for my barrenness, for the bride-price money he had wasted on the defective good I had now become. But Agu was deaf to my voice and blind to my tears. His hands continued to descend on my head, pulling clumps off my scalp. His feet shot home countless goals on my body. Soon, my screams turned to whimpers and my voice grew hoarse in my throat. When eventually his arms grew weary and his breathing laboured from exhaustion, Agu dropped his belt on the floor and matched out of the room in the same death-silence with which he had carried out the prolonged attack on my person.

As for myself, I was at the gates of mental darkness and mortal hell, my vision hazy from dizziness and pain. Choking back the countless hiccups that threatened to kill my breathing, I crawled my way back to my room, bright blood stains marking the white linoleum floor of the corridor. I stumbled my way to the wall mirror, fearful, yet desperate to see the damage to my person.

The Unclean

The scream that escaped my lips at the image the mirror returned to me was louder than any I had made while the damage was wreaked on it. I shut my eyes tight, fighting to blank out the swellings, the open cuts, the blood dripping from every opening in my face. But I couldn't shut out the agonising throbbing in my body, the shame and the fury. Most of all, I couldn't shut out the sudden hate that burnt in my heart like a bush fire gone wild.

***

That night, and many more nights over the course of several months, Agu vented his fury and frustration on my body with his fists and everything he could lay his stumpy hands on. His three obese sisters who shared the house with us, took equal liberties on my person, till my loathed light skin was repainted with a collage of blues, reds and blacks.

On numerous occasions, I was kept locked up in my room, guarded by the mammoth sisters and numerous house-helps. The only times they were let off their guard duty were on the nights my husband came to claim his conjugal rights on my body, a brutal ritual carried out in silence and darkness, leaving me with a feeling of defilement and shame.

Eventually, I could bear the abuse no longer. One day when Agu left for his monthly trade trips to the Muslim north, I made my escape back to my father's village. I caught the mammy-wagon bus that ferried traders to Onitsha Market once a week, usually on a Friday morning. I hunched low in my seat, head bowed, as the rickety bus rumbled along the potholed road, spewing black smoke into the air, its horn blaring out with nerve-wracking regularity as if to say, "look at me, I can talk, I can shriek!" Its manic racket fed the wild emotions that burned in my heart like a Harmattan bush-fire.

A mounting rage engulfed my body, fury at what that horrid midget and his vile sisters had done to me.

The Unclean

Just wait till I tell Papa, I thought over and over as the bus rumbled its bumpy way to my village. I pulled my headscarf almost to my nose like a Muslim woman, desperate to hide my latest bruises from the other passengers. I did not want anyone to see my shame… *save my family*. For them, there would be no pride, no humiliation. For my family, I would bare my very soul.

Chapter Five

I arrived at my father's village a few hours later and walked the short distance to his compound, my eyes fixed to the ground to avoid recognition. As I walked through the low metal gate of our compound, I saw Papa's Raleigh bicycle perched against the whitewashed wall of our L-shaped bungalow. The sight of that bicycle flooded my mind with memories, bitter-sweet nostalgia that stung my eyes with salty water.

My feet grew sudden wings as I raced the last few yards to our front door. I pulled my scarf from my head, wincing in pain as the cloth connected with my bruises, dislodging fresh scabs. I heard the sound of approaching footsteps and felt the sudden tears spill down my cheeks, tears of self-pity, relief, pain and anger all mixed into one loud bawl.

The Unclean

My sister, Gono, opened the door. She took one look at my battered, tear-streaked face and started howling. She just stood at the open door, her hands pressed tightly against her ears, staring at me with wide streaming eyes, her bare feet stamping on the floor like the frenzied dance of the *Adamma* masquerade. Except her dance wasn't one of joy or excitement, but rage and pain, a pain I knew was as biting as mine because of the great love she bore for me.

Behind her, I saw my brother, Ibe, craning his neck and trying to see what the ruckus was all about. His eyes widened as he took in my bruises before hurrying away without a word to me. Mama rushed out, Ibe fast on her heels, his eyes gleaming with sly excitement.

"What's all this foolishness about? Don't you know your father is having his afternoon siesta?' Mama scolded, pushing Gono away from me. Then, just like Gono, her eyes widened as she too took in my battered face.

She threw her arms wide into the air, her eyes raised to the low ceiling in an attitude of supplication. 'Jesu!' she shouted, making a quick sign of the cross before leading me by the arm into Papa's presence, her breathing hard and fast.

'Papa Ibe! Papa Ibe, wake up,' she shook Papa's shoulder with urgent hands. I felt the slight irritation of old stir in my heart at the usurpation of my right. I was the first born and prior to Ibe's arrival, Papa had been known as "Papa Desee" by everyone. But with Ibe's birth, him being a son and all, that coveted status was taken from me and given to the wretched sod.

As Papa slowly awakened, Mama went over to her armless chair, folding her arms over her bosom. She had the look of a guard dog awaiting the "attack" order from its master. It was a look that filled my heart with a warm glow. I felt like a child whose big brother was going to thrash the school bully for picking on him. Papa forced his eyes apart, his movements sluggish, confused. A look of annoyance clouded his face as he kissed his teeth in an angry hiss.

'Can't a man get any rest in his own house?' he grumbled, stretching his hand for his snuffbox by his side table. His mood didn't lighten any when his eyes settled on me. I could see the dark brown tobacco stain at the bottom of his nostrils, just above his lips. I felt a strong urge to wipe it with a cloth… *a hankie, something… anything.*

For some incomprehensible reason, I couldn't bear the sight of that dark tobacco stain under Papa's nose. I had more pressing problems, yet, that unsightly dot overshadowed everything else to such an extent that I even forgot to curtsy to my grandfather's grave in the centre of the living room as was customary. In fact, for several confused seconds, I couldn't recall why Mama had brought me into the parlour till I heard her discreet cough beside me.

I tore my gaze from Papa's dirty nostrils and dragged my mind back to my troubles. Mama nodded at me to speak. Once again, I could not hold back my tears as I narrated my marital woes to Papa, showing him the wreck Agu had made of my body. I was angry, shouting and gesticulating wildly, as I recounted the litany of abuse Agu and his people had inflicted on my person. It was as if my voice, long buried, had been given a new life; as if my pride, long murdered in Ukari, had been reanimated within the safety of my father's house.

I wanted vengeance. Someone had to pay for what I had suffered. Someone needed to feel the pain I had felt. That someone was Agu, my so-called husband and his three fat sisters. I wanted Papa to round up a band of youths from the masquerade age group, those muscle-chested boy-men who could beat the hard-skinned drums from dusk to dawn without tiring. They were our village braves, self-appointed guardians of the community, who made it their duty to ensure no crimes occurred on their watch or went unavenged when committed. I wanted Papa to take those tough boys to Ukari and trash the skin off that midget trader and his obese sisters. I wanted Agu and his family to cry as I had cried, to feel the burning of birch, the pounding of fists, the cutting of flesh, just as I had done. I wanted them to be familiar with the tangy taste of blood and snot, which no food, no matter how sweet, would ever wash from their taste buds for eternity.

But most of all, I wanted my old room back; that small book-choked room I'd shared with my sister once upon a blissful time, before I was driven from its womb-like warmth to the cold soulless Hades of Agu's house.

Papa listened to me in total silence, his dark face inscrutable, unyielding. He kept piling tobacco powder into his nostrils all the while I spoke, his eyes boring into mine as I talked. Slowly, insidiously, a sense of unease started to creep into my heart. My voice began to falter, my stomach tightening into knots. Looking into the hard blackness of Papa's eyes, something told me that he would not save me from my matrimonial hell.

I was not mistaken.

Papa looked at Ibe as if to say, "Take good heed of this crucial lesson for when you have troublesome daughters of your own", before turning back to me. A deep frown creased his forehead as he piled his nostrils with yet more tobacco powder.

'You are your husband's chattel now,' Papa said, fixing me with a fierce look that would brook no arguments. 'Nobody can come between a man and his wife. Whatever food they dish out to you should be eaten with endurance and gratitude. It is bad enough that you have shamed this family with your barrenness without adding the dishonour of a divorce. Where do you expect me to find the money to refund him the dowry he paid on your head should you return, eh? Do you want me to sell my *Ọgọdọ*, my precious loincloth, to raise money to refund your dowry? Go, return to your husband and cease your whinging and childish behaviour. Kindly remember that you're the *Ada,* my first daughter. Your sister looks to you to set a good example. Do not let her down.'

My father waved me away from his presence. I cast a wild look at my mother, unable to comprehend, to accept what my ears had heard. Surely, Mama would not stand by and let this happen to me; surely, she would talk to my father, convince him that I must never return to Ukari under any circumstance. I was even prepared to forego revenge, to let Agu get away with his crime if I were certain I would never see him or his accursed village again.

But my mother shrugged and looked away. My mother would not meet my eyes. The guard-dog look left her face and instead, I saw her lips curl down in that familiar manner I remembered from childhood, that silent message that said, "Your father knows best. You have to do as he says". But this was no longer some petty quarrel between siblings, some childish ploy for attention. This was a matter of life and death… *my life, her daughter's death!* Surely, she would not fold her hands and watch me die. She was a married woman like me. My father had never treated her as Agu treated me. She had to do something, say something to change Papa's mind. She was my mother, *my mother!*

'Mama!' My cry bore the weight of my pain, my terror. It forced itself from the depths of my soul, insisting on being heard. But my mother remained silent, a silent partner in her husband's crime. For in my mind, what they were doing was criminal, heartless, even evil. *How could two people who conceived and gave life to me calmly hand me over to my killer for thirty pieces of dowry silver?'* I thought, fighting to control my tears. In my mind, they were no better than Judas Iscariot. In fact, they were worse that Emeka, that childless village drunk, whom rumour had it sold his own daughter to the slave traders in his previous incarnation, resulting in his present curse. Five wives down the line and Emeka was still childless. His last wife finally ran off with a Mami-wagon driver and promptly had a child by her lover. In my present predicament, I cared little if Emeka was innocent or guilty as charged. To me, he was the embodiment of everything my parents had suddenly become – treachery and betrayal.

With weary resignation, I turned away from my parents and walked out of the parlour, setting my face into the stoic mask of the example-giver, calm, patient and forbearing, just like a pious nun. After all, as my father said, I was the first daughter and my sister expected me to set a good example.

Thankfully, my father was wrong.

My sister, Gono, did not expect any such martyr-like example from me. She took one look at my set features and rushed over to me. Her tears re-awakened my own. She clasped my shuddering body in her arms as I poured out my despair to her ears, the only ears that truly heard my pain. My body shuddered with the force of my tears and anger.

'Bastards! Men are all bastards! Useless lumps of pig shit!' Gono raged. 'I wish I were a man. By God, I will reincarnate as a man in my next life and then we'll see who calls the shots. Look at that idiot, Ibe. Already he's a replica of Papa, an *akologholi,* a useless little jerk with no brain cells in his big head. He's not a child anymore, for Christ's sake. He's almost seventeen years now, the same age you were when you married that dwarf. If he were a real man, he would go to Ukari and trash the living daylight out of that short bastard that calls himself your husband. But don't worry sis, don't cry. Everything will be okay soon, you'll see.'

The Unclean

I hugged my little sister tightly, unwilling to separate our bond. I was allowed to spend the night under my father's roof on the proviso that no one found out that I'd done so without my husband's permission and that I left before the crow of the rooster the next day.

It was with a weary heart that I dressed up at the crack of dawn to make my feet-dragging way back to my husband's house. I did not exchange a word with my father as I left his house for my return journey to Ukari. I managed to smuggle out a few books from my old room - Jane Eyre, David Copperfield, and The Water Babies. My books reminded me of what had been and what could have been had Queen Ill-fortune not dealt me such a cruel hand and a bad father. They evoked memories of happier times and to an extent, salvaged my sanity.

I felt a strong closeness to Jane Eyre in particular, whose wretchedness and ultimate triumph filled my heart with hope of a better destiny in some distant future. And just before I got on the Mami-wagon taking me back to Ukari village, Mama ran out and pushed a piece of paper into my hand before rushing back into the house again, ever fearful of incurring my father's wrath for encouraging my perceived rebellion. It was too dark to read the contents of the crumbled piece of paper as the sun was still to chase the moon back to its cold realm.

When I finally read the short note, written in the familiar dear hand of my sister, Gono, it contained the address of a famed Spiritualist, Pastor Brother Ezekiel of the *Aladura* spiritualist church. My sister's bold calligraphy penned Mama's wishes for me to visit the powerful pastor without delay, as he was the key to my problems. It was an instruction I was happy to obey. I was at the end of my endurance and ready to dine with Lucifer himself if he would free me from my marital yoke.

Chapter Six

Pastor Brother Ezekiel proved to be everything I had hoped for and more. He identified and broke all my ancestral curses, binding the demons of infertility with chicken and goat sacrifices, a full body wash in consecrated water, mixed with the blood of my monthly curse and a burnt offering of my shaved pubic hair, the pages of the book of Psalms and a new-born's umbilical cord. I sold my best *Ashoke* ceremonial gown to raise the money to buy the last item from a private midwife and it was worth every last *Naira* note in the end.

Pastor Brother Ezekiel was possessed with the spirit of Arch-angel Michael on the night of my spiritual cleansing at his *Aladura* church. He spoke in tongues, wondrous and mysterious holy words that sent my senses into righteous ecstasy. And when Arch-

Angel Michael possessed my trembling body, filling my womb with the holy seeds of fertility, I knew that my sorrows were finally at an end. Queen Ill-fortune had finally met her match in the all-conquering angel of our omnipotent creator, the Arch-Angel Michael himself!

***

I gave birth to my son exactly nine months to the date of my holy cleansing and my husband aptly named him Chukwuebuka, meaning, "God is great!" Everyone called him Ebuka, the shortened version of his name. Ebuka's birth healed the pain of my childless marriage, four years of humiliation, abuse and contempt. My sisters-in-law, overnight, metamorphosed from Lucifer to St Peter, guarding my well-being and that of my son with the same zeal with which St Peter guarded the gates of heaven.

Gone were the harsh words, the accusations, the bitter recriminations, the beatings. Even Uzo, the worst of the rotund three, mellowed her hate, bringing me freshly-made *Akamu*, mushy corn pap, for the baby. I knew it was her way of making up for all the gossip she had spread about my *Mamiwata* mermaid ancestry and accursed infertility. I was ready to accept her peace-offerings. After all, I had been vindicated, made triumphant over Queen Ill-fortune, finally secure in my marital home with a husband who had not lifted a violent hand on my person since the birth of his heir.

Agu threw a lavish party for the baptism of our son. Father O'Keefe officiated the ceremony and consecrated Ebuka with holy water as he read out his two names, Chukwuebuka (which he struggled to pronounce) and Michael, which he proclaimed with loud confidence. I was lavished with new clothes and jewellery for the event and my father's face was full of smiles at the baptism party. I had finally done him proud.

Sadly, Pastor Brother Ezekiel was not invited despite being the instrument of my miracle. Father O'Keefe would have frowned at my interaction with that segment of the Christian fraternity. The *Aladura* spiritual church was still viewed with suspicion by the Catholic Church due to its practise of mixing Christianity with local traditions. Instead, I sent Pastor Brother Ezekiel a handsome gift in an envelope after the ceremony. I could afford it; the guests had been very generous with their donations and money gifts for the new baby.

**

As the months went by and Ebuka grew stronger, Agu became kinder to me. He began addressing me with the endearment, *Nkem,* meaning, "my own". I was treated with respect by the villagers and addressed by the proud title, *Mama Ebuka*. I was now a mother. I had fulfilled my calling as a woman, a daughter and a wife. I had finally earned my place in society and gained acceptance amongst my husband's people.

I soon grew fat on a diet of contentment and pride. As our people say, a beggar who never dreamt of becoming a king will drown himself in ivory amulets from his heels to his chest, so that no one will be in doubt of his importance. I was as crass as that stupid beggar, boasting of the beauty, the strength, the cleverness of my son, Ebuka. My eyes were haughty with pride, my voice loud in confidence, my mien complacent in contentment, as I marinated in my own sauce of arrogance.

Until the day Queen Ill-fortune paid me an unexpected and devastating visit, wreaking deadly vengeance on me for my contempt of her might. It was only after she left my house that I realised that the moon was a perfect swollen melon. In my pride and folly, I had ceased to keep score, to watch, to follow and dread the changes in the cycle of that omen-moon.

The Unclean

Until that fatal eve of the New Yam festival, that terrible weltering afternoon when the house-maid brought in the small, lifeless body of my son, Ebuka, his features swollen and distorted by the venom of the evil viper, *Echieteka*, whose fearsome name meant, "tomorrow is too far to live". Queen Ill-fortune had dealt me the deadliest of blows yet, and her moon stayed fat in the sky for several nights to mock my sorrow.

***

The clanswomen said that I would not let go of my son's lifeless body; that I clung to him like a bat to its cave, fighting all that tried to prise him from my arms with the strength of ten mad women. They said that even after I had finally been restrained by the men of the clan, my relentless keening had kept the inhabitants of the surrounding compounds awake for several nights. According to them, the mourning food cooked for me by the village women went uneaten, while my body withered and wasted with the speed of my mind's deterioration.

I remembered none of it. I remembered nothing beyond the cold, cold body of my beautiful son... and the callus laughter of Queen Ill-fortune ringing in my brain, day and night. The women of the clan beat my housemaid to near-death. Not because of her dereliction of duty resulting in my innocent son picking up the deadly snake with his bare hands while she scampered atop the mango trees in search of the sweet ripe fruits.

They beat her instead for breaking the most sacred of taboos - letting my eyes behold the lifeless body of my son. "What self-respecting Igbo person doesn't know that a parent's eyes must never see the corpse of their deceased child?" They shrieked, as they thrashed the sobbing girl to an inch of her life. Such an abomination would bring untold misfortune to the entire clan. Not only had my eyes beheld my dead son, but I had also held his lifeless body in my arms for several hours, ensuring that Queen Ill-fortune's dreaded attention had been caught and drawn to the entire clan!

Ha! What did I care? As if that terrible deity's attention had ever left my side. Let her visit as much as she likes; go ahead and spread her dark favours on Agu's family and entire clan. Let them know my misery, share my pain and know what it is to play host to that malevolent visitor.

My son was dead. No one would ever again call me *"Mami"* in that sweet baby voice. Arch-Angel Michael had been roundly defeated by Queen Ill-fortune. I was soul-weary, tired of resisting my fate. Whatever evil I had done in my previous existence had to be paid for in full in my present life. I had now paid my dues. Ebuka was gone. I had lost everything. All I wanted was out, freedom to join my son in the dark, cold embrace of death. I knew there would be peace in the sandy warmth of the grave. But at least, I would be with my beloved son, and hopefully, in my next reincarnation, I would finally return with a good *Chi.*

***

By the time my mind found its way back to the land of the sane, it was too late for me to find my son. Search as I could, ask as I dared, no one would show me where the tiny corpse of my son lay. All I knew was that he was buried in *Ajọ-ọfia,* the bad bush, a barren and desolate stretch of landscape inhabited by the cursed bodies of the unclean, those who died a cursed death. Their bodies were discarded in the bad bush, unmourned and forgotten - suicides, murderers, witches and wizards, night-flyers, poisoners, victims of lightning, mothers who died giving birth, widows who died while in mourning, children who died before their parents and people who were judged and destroyed by The Tree of Truth.

Nothing grew in *Ajọ-ọfia* but giant anthills, housing massive termites bloated from gorging on the corpses of the damned. It was no place for my innocent beautiful son, a laughing and happy child once beloved and cherished by all. His little red shoes still lay hidden in my room, buried deep in my *Adu, a* weaved garment basket that held my expensive wrappers. My Adu kept the tiny shoes safe from the evil and prying eyes of the clanswomen. They would burn those beautiful shoes with the same brutal speed with which they'd burnt all his clothing, wipe out all traces of his existence with the same cold and ruthless efficiency they'd cast away his tiny body in *Ajọ-ọfia,* his grave unmarked by stone or cross, ensuring his name would be forgotten by mankind for all eternity and his spirit would never find its way back to its home to reincarnate amongst its people.

And for what crime? For dying from a poisonous snake bite? For dying too young before his time, before his parents? What had my innocent baby done to deserve such evil from the entire clan and village? I wanted to find his grave, to visit that accursed bush where his body lay discarded like bat-eaten mangoes, rancid and worthless. But my cowardly woman's heart feared the vengeful ghosts of the accursed dead that shared the bad bush with my little son. No matter how many *Hail Marys* I chanted, how many bottles of holy water I drank, how many wooden and metal crucifixes I collected or how many *Jigida* charmed amulets I wore around my waist to ward off evil spirits, my courage refused to reside in my heart and I could never make the long and fearful journey to my child's last resting place and mark his unhallowed grave with a mother's loving touch.

Chapter Seven

(Ukari Forest – 2am)

Agu's eyes, closed by death, suddenly fly apart, staring their bloody glare into my eyes, eyes stretched to my ears by heart-thumping terror. My limbs melt, my breathing stops, my heart falls to my stomach as I fight to retain my sanity in the midst of the latest horror that has descended upon me in this forest of the damned. As I struggle to revive my feet, to flee from the zombie ghoul on the raffia mat, his right arm, rotting with peeling flesh, shoots up and grabs my throat, squeezing out my life with a strength and malignancy that is beyond the realms of the living.

I scream - yell - as I struggle to escape from the vengeful decaying demon that had once been my husband. But my voice is silent, my cries swallowed by my terror. I see the stinking, bloated carcass slowly rise from the forest floor, the raffia mat clinging to its pus-seeping skin. The stench of decay and rank is overpowering, almost stealing the air from my lungs. That bristly and mottled organ is hard against my thighs, rough and painful. IT *demands forceful entrance to my secret place, still bruised and hurting from all its previous assaults. The hands on my throat tighten their grip, squeezing, hurting, till I feel the darkness of death pounding in my brain, seeking entry.*

Yet, even as death waits impatiently for my soul, even as I feel the deadly pressure on my throat, something in me refuses to give in, to give up without fighting for the one thing that still belongs to me – my life.

As pathetic as it is, it's still my own to keep or destroy. I know that if I don't flee, find a way to break through the charmed salt boundary set around me by the witchdoctors, my soul will become entwined with Agu's for all eternity.

For that is the fate of all murderers. Their lives are destined to be taken by their victim's ghosts, to be joined to their victims in death, like co-joined twins, condemned to an eternity of vengeful justice at the hands of these earth-bound spirits.

Blessed Virgin, spare my soul! *I do not want to become a restless dead amongst my other curses and for all eternity, denied the chance of a better reincarnation. I begin to struggle with a desperation born of mind-killing terror, kicking, scratching, screaming, shoving.*

My eyes fly awake and I rise to the sound of silence, a graveside stillness that makes me wish for the oblivion of death by its sheer soundless terror. My heart is thudding so loudly I fear I will faint and then truly be damned. With small whimpering cries, I scramble away on bruised knees from Agu's bloated corpse, pulling myself to the very edge of the salt ring that has me chained to The Tree of Truth, shoulders hunched, my arms clasped tightly around my raised knees.

I stare – peer intently into Agu's swollen face, searching, looking for any sign of the terrifying animation I'd witnessed in my nightmare. Do his eyes flicker? Do I see his nose twitch? Surely, I hear something that sounds as soft as dandelion pores, a pungent exhalation that blows a sudden chill on my exposed flesh!

I force my eyes to take a brave peep at the jutting monster between his naked thighs, still throbbing in its knobbled evil, the undead tentacle in the lump of fetid rottenness that was my husband. It pulsates with a living strength that defies the rancid body that houses it. Oh Mary Mother of God! *Will IT never die? Will IT never wilt? Will IT ever let me go?*

Pulling my hair, tangled in filthy clumps on my scalp, I feel like hammering a stone into my skull to punish my brain for its stupidity. How could I have allowed my guard to slip, to give in to sleep, allowing Agu's vengeful spirit to attempt the possession of my body and chain me to him in eternal servitude? God knows he has enough to be vengeful about. My stupidity and desperation had cost him among other things, his life.

If only I hadn't been so desperate, so frightened. But what mother can hear the pitiful cries of her child and turn a deaf ear? Everything would have been alright if only Ebuka hadn't died, if Enu hadn't come into our family, if I had stayed away from that demon, Ogbunigwe. If only I hadn't been so foolish, so……

Chapter Eight

Eight months after the death of my son, Agu took a second wife, Enu. Older than me by several years, she was young enough to provide the male child to replace my late son and ensure the perpetuity of our husband's bloodline. Enu also had the advantage of being a local woman, born in Ukari of Ukari parentage. I was considered a tall woman but Enu towered over me by several fingers. She was a woman of mammoth proportions. Seeing her together with our husband for the first time was a sight I would never forget. Agu could have easily been mistaken for her son but for that strutting walk of his, peculiar to all pocketsize dictators. I would have burst out in a maniac's laughter had my situation not been so dire.

As soon as the wretched woman swaggered her way into our house, Agu threw me out of my room and consigned me to the back quarters of the house, the section reserved for the domestic helps. Enu took over ownership of my room and all the privileges of the main wife, from the domestic helps to the shopping and food management. I couldn't tell which was worse – the scorn of my husband and his sisters or the indifferent pity and contempt of the house-servants, who soon sucked up their way into the new mistress' favour with tales of my anguish.

I would see them gathered, sniggering, whispering into their new mistress's ears. My ears would burn as Enu hissed at my back the way one would hiss at a house pest. I was her senior in rank, the first wife, but our husband had stripped me of my rank and the respect that went with it. At best, I was no higher than the house servants now.

As time went by, I lost all interest in reading, even when the opportunity presented itself. What was the use? Where had all my education landed me? Not as a doctor's or lawyer's wife as Papa had anticipated. I was instead in the back quarters of a man who couldn't string together two words of English if his life depended on it. The sooner I resigned myself to the reality of my life and accepted myself as a village minion, the better I would adapt to my new life.

***

Less than a year into her marriage, Enu fulfilled expectations with the birth of a son, whose striking resemblance to our husband was confirmed in his name, Nwanna, meaning, his father's son. On the night of Nwanna's birth, Queen Ill-fortune's gleeful laughter rang so loudly in my head I feared I would lose my sanity.

At a point, I cried out in anguish, uncaring what ears might hear my torment - *Please, great deity, leave me alone… forget my existence as the morning skies forget the night stars. Discard me as the tree sheds its dead leaves. Have you not toyed enough with my life so that I am but a wretched husk of humanity, worthless, insignificant, a mere shadow? Why continue noticing this pathetic lump of wretchedness? Why...why?*

I swallowed the hard knot behind my throat and masked my face with celebratory smiles at the wondrous arrival of our husband's heir, Nwanna, even as I sensed the malice behind the smiles of the clanswomen, heard the velvet spite behind their solicitous enquiries about my well-being–

"*Nwunye-anyi*, our wife, did you spend too much time with your kitchen smoke? Look, it has brought charcoal redness to your eyes, you poor woman!"

However, there was nothing I could do to shield the evidence of my pain, try as I could. My reddened eyes remained puffed with unfinished tears, ready to shed my agony at the slightest excuse. Once, I had known the bliss of holding a child in my arms, suckling his little head on my tender breasts, his skin soft, silky to the touch, his voice beautiful and sweet when he called me *"Mami"*. Now, I had nothing, *nothing.* I would never again know the glory of motherhood.

The same villagers that had once treated me with respect, now scorned me with indifference. Every honour now went to Enu and her new son. Our husband had ceased to know me as a wife from the day my son died. Now he had another wife and son, I had become an outcast of both man and the gods.

***

One night, a year to the birth of Nwanna, I awoke to the sound of a child's cries outside my window. It was mournful and muted, yet at the same time, piercing and insistent. I sat up on my bed, its loose springs squeaking out in protest. The cries stopped - just for a few seconds - then resumed with louder intensity.

A cold chill coated my skin in goosebumps. I knew that sound, recognised the distinctive wail of a new-born infant. *Bush-Baby! Oh sweet Mary, save me!* I quickly crossed myself, my heart racing like a wild antelope. The Bush-baby is a nocturnal primate with a child's fingers, which mimics the cries of a new-born baby. It is a cursed creature, sent by enemies to cast evil spells on unsuspecting people. When sent to a woman, it kills all affections the husband has for her, ensuring she'll never become pregnant and have a child. Tricking unwary women with their infant-like cries, these evil creatures assume the form of wicked goblins, raping the women and biting off their toes after the vile act so that people know what had taken place. Consequently, all future children born by the molested women must be killed and buried at the *Ajọ-ọfia* to ensure the *Bush-Baby* curse is destroyed.

And now, this terrible creature had turned up outside my window! I stumbled through the darkness to my window, to make sure the latch was firmly secured before returning to my bed, my heart thudding in unbridled terror. I *knew* who had sent me the Bush-Baby – Enu, my husband's second wife. Not content with taking my husband, my bedroom and my status, she now wished to inflict the vilest of all curses on me by having me molested by the goblin Bush-Baby. *Oh Holy Mary mother of God! Would my travails never end?*

I spent the rest of the night in wakeful misery, listening to the incessant cries of that evil abomination till Agu's prize cockerel crowed in the dawn and the unholy cries finally ceased.

For three more nights, the accursed *Bush-Baby* outside my window tormented my sleep. And on the fourth night, it entered my room.

***

I awoke to the familiar child-like wails, feeling a terror grip my heart beyond anything I've ever felt since the death of my son. The cries ceased as soon as I opened my eyes. *Something was wrong, very wrong; bad.* The unnatural stillness in my room was heavy with a waiting quality that made the darkness a solid malignant mass. Covered in cold sweat, I fumbled for the box of matches to light my kerosene lantern.

In the thin light of the lamp, I picked out a sudden movement near my *Adu,* the high basket that contained my special clothes, reserved for weddings and Sunday service. Something scuttled to the back of the *Adu*, something the size of a dog, yet faster in motion than any dog I had ever seen.

Then it cried, a sound so piercing and terrible that my heart froze. *Bush-Baby! Oh Holy Maria! Jesus!* My limbs turned to mushy food and my urine sac filled to explosion. *What to do? Oh Jesus save me!* There was no escape through my door as the *Adu* stood behind the wooden door on the inside of my bedroom. My eyes darted wildly around the room, looking for something, anything, to defend myself. The gleaming silver of my crucifix on the small table beckoned like an angel's halo. I reached out my hand to it and froze. Cold, skeletal claws crawled down my back.

The Unclean

Ebuka, my beautiful, sweet son, stood in front of me; Ebuka, naked as the day he was born, his skin caked in the dirty mud of his unhallowed grave! I wanted to scream…I think I screamed. Then my mind died.

***

I awoke, drenched in cold water, surrounded by Enu, our husband, the fat sisters and the house-servants. Enu held an empty bucket in her hand. I figured she must have doused me in cold water to bring me out of my faint. For a few seconds, my shame dulled my memory, especially when I saw the fury in Agu's eyes. Then recollection returned with terrifying panic.

'Ebbbbbuka!' I stuttered, struggling to speak through the terror that still held my heart in its grip. I cast wild looks around my room as I struggled to my feet, my wet cloths clinging to my skin, bringing shivers to my entire body. 'Ebuka... where's Ebuka? He's here...he's back...'

'*Chei! Tufia!* Heaven forbid evil! The woman is crazy again!' Enu shouted, snapping her fingers to ward off being infected by my lunacy, a cold smirk on her face. '*Onye-ishi,* when are you going to get rid of this mad woman, eh? It's not fair that our peace is ruined by her. Your son, Nwanna, needs his sleep, which this crazy woman won't let him have. I think...'

Agu raised his hand, cutting off Enu's tirade with that single gesture. At the same time, he waved away his sisters and the wide-eyed house-helps, his cold eyes fixed on me all the while.

'Return to your room,' he said to Enu without taking his eyes from me. I saw a look of rebellion flash across Enu's eyes as she hesitated. 'Go! Now!' Agu barked. Enu didn't need a second warning. Despite her mammoth size, I've heard her loud yelps on a few occasions, as a result of Agu's fists. I'll say it for our husband, he was indiscriminate in his violence, even if I got the lion share.

As the door slammed behind her, Agu approached me, his steps silent, deliberate. I huddled closer to the bed-post, pulling my pillow close, anything to ward off the blows I knew were coming my way.

'So…your son returned to you, did he?' Agu's voice was soft, dangerous. 'You dare mock me with a name that should never be mentioned in my house! You stupid, stupid woman.'

My pillow was useless, as were my cries for mercy. Agu rained his fury on my body, my head, my face, leaving me a bloody, crumbled wreck on the floor when he was done.

The next night, when my son returned to me, I knew better than to scream or faint. I fought my terror and spoke to my son. By the time we were done talking, all my former fears had disappeared. The following night, I had a basin of clean water and new clothes waiting in my room, together with his tiny red shoes I had saved since his death.

I washed the grave-mud and death odour off him, oiled his body with palm-kernel oil, combed his thick hair and dressed him up with his new clothes and the red shoes, which still fitted perfectly. Then I carried him in my arms and rocked him till sleep came to me.

When I awoke the next morning, Ebuka was gone and his clothes and little red shoes lay abandoned on my bed. I felt the tears choke my throat at my new loss, a loss now magnified by the brief bliss of motherhood I had experienced in the night. Suddenly, the pain from Agu's brutality on my body returned with throbbing intensity. I had felt nothing since my son returned to me and his disappearance re-awakened all my dormant pains, both mental and physical.

For the first time, I contemplated suicide. *Surely, death was better than this earthly torment!* But Our Virgin Mother must have heard my prayers and sympathised with my pain, the same pain she too had experienced at the death of her son on the cross of Calgary. Because on the following night, my son came back to me.

Ebuka entered my bedroom naked, again caked in filthy mud from his unhallowed grave, with that foul smell of decay still clinging to him despite all my scrubbing and washing. I did not care if he were coated in human and animal excrement. I welcomed him into my arms with indescribable joy. Once again, I carried out the loving chore of cleansing and dressing him, now secure in the knowledge that he would be back the following night, till my love held him back for good and he lost the urge to go back to his unhallowed grave in *Ajọ-ọfia.*

***

So began my second phase of motherhood. I nursed and loved my dead baby who neither ate nor stayed beyond the light of dawn. No matter what delicacies I offered him, Ebuka would never take a single bite nor drink a sip of water. His eyes remained open through the night and his cold little body would never soak the warmth from my cradling arms. But he was happy to be together with his loving *Mami* again. Even though he never chuckled anymore in that carefree way of his living days, his steady gaze and seeking hands told me he was contented to be with his *Mami.*

And me? My steps grew lighter and my face glowed with ecstasy. I noticed the suspicious looks of the household, the whispers – *"It's the madness... she's too far gone now for help! But* Onye-ishi *won't do anything about her till she starts running around naked. Just make sure you keep Nwanna away from her. I don't want her tainting my son with her lunacy.'*

Enu voiced her thoughts in a voice loud enough for the whole village to hear, stumping all over the place, her eyes sending me daggers. *Ha! As if I cared for her precious son!* I had my own son with me again and that was enough for me

But I wasn't enough for Ebuka, though. He started asking me to bring him back for good. He was lonely and sad in *Ajo-ofia*. The cursed soil kept coughing up his corpse, rejecting his body as the humans had rejected it. He was an unclean, a child that had died a cursed death before his parents, doomed to a restless grave in Ajo-ofia. It had taken him years to find his way back to our house, a miracle in itself, considering the remoteness of his gravesite. He missed me desperately and wanted to remain with me, but he could not return for good till he was reincarnated back to us.

I knew Ebuka's only chance of reincarnation lay with me getting pregnant, enabling him to return through my new pregnancy and birth. But how could I make that happen when our husband no longer touched me as a wife? The urge to return to Pastor Brother Ezekiel was great. After all, I had him to thank for

Ebuka's birth in the first place. But I resisted that temptation with the stubbornness of a Christmas ram being dragged to the butcher's knife. I dared not incur the wrath of Queen Ill-fortune again, who seemed now to have forgotten my existence.

But our people have a saying – "To fight a demon, you need the devil." Queen Ill-fortune was a demon deity and I would need a demon-savvy witchdoctor to aid my cause and bring back my son to life.

Chapter Nine

I visited Ogbunigwe's hut at midnight of the next full moon. He would only see supplicants at that specific time. My heart quaked at the sight of the swollen moon, knowing that Queen Ill-fortune was at her most mischievous on such nights. Yet, I had no choice. If I was to have my son back for good, then the only way was to brave the evil deity and seek the famed medicine man, Ogbunigwe, meaning, "he that kills in multitudes".

Ogbunigwe was as fierce-faced as his reputation stated, tall, marble-featured, coal-skinned and bloody of eyes. The great medicine man was dressed in nothing but a loin-cloth and multiple amulets and charms. His body was knife-carved with intricate *Nsibidi* designs too mysterious for me to decipher. His voice when he spoke to me, was stentorian, deep, yet raspy, full of authority and ancient knowledge. The aura of menace about him terrified me even more than the macabre place he lived, set deep in the forest, and littered with numerous human skulls and animal carcasses.

I felt an icy chill litter my body in goosebumps. The urge to turn around and flee was strong but my feet were rooted in the soil by terror. I had come too far now to back out and despite everything, my son was my everything and for him, I would dance with the lord of hell himself, Lucifer.

All around the shrine, the metallic smell of blood was strong, overpowering, coupled with another strange odour I could not fathom. As I stepped through the low door of Ogbunigwe's hut, I noticed that the cement flooring of the room was polished with blood. Briefly, the thought flickered in my mind - *What will Father O'Keefe think of me if he knew where I was?* I couldn't believe that I, Desdemona, once an aspiring teacher and a devout Catholic, had now descended to this level of fetishness. I waved the thought away – *We are all what our* Chi *decides for us. Who can say what is right and what is wrong? After all, didn't King Saul himself visit the Witch of Endor in the Bible and spoke to God's prophet, Samuel?*

As I looked around Ogbunigwe's gloomy hut, I recalled my first and last visit to another of his kind. Next to Ogbunigwe, the decrepit charlatan my sister-in-law had taken me to visit all those many years gone, seemed like an ignorant apprentice, a total novice in the art of wizardry.

I bowed my head low and fell to my knees before the great Juju-man.

'Great One, please, hear the pleas of your handmaiden,' I could neither control the tremor in my voice nor the quake in my body. 'My husband no longer touches me as a wife, and I am a woman without a child. My childbearing years are shortening, and my departed son is now a restless dead. He cannot reincarnate back to his clan without a pregnancy in my belly. Help me, great and wise One. Give me the pregnancy I seek. Give me back my son. Chain my husband to my side, so that my belly may once more swell with the seeds of a child and the bloodline is preserved,' my tears flowed unchecked as I beat my chest repeatedly with my fists.

Ogbunigwe was silent for several minutes, staring down at me from his great height, his face inscrutable, like the jagged rocks surrounding his abode.

'Are you prepared to pay the price?' His voice was low, deep, terrible.

'I have saved enough money,' I said, reaching to the lumpy knot at the edge of my wrapper, where my folded *Naira* notes were hidden.

'Foolish woman! Keep your money,' his hand waved away my offering with disdain. 'Listen with your ears and pay heed to my words. I repeat, are you prepared to pay the price?' He punctuated every word like one speaking to a silly child.

Then I knew. And yet I did not know. I suddenly recalled another saying of my people – *"never dine with the devil without a very long spoon, in case you need to make a speedy escape"*. A favour from the devil always came with a price in blood. *But whose blood? Whose death?* I could already sense the presence of Queen Ill-fortune at my side, mocking me, laughing at my dilemma. Her glee decided me. I was done with being the play-thing of the queen of misery.

'I am ready, Great One,' my voice was resolute, with no signs of its earlier tremor. 'I am ready to pay the price.'

'On your head be it. Before the gods, I wash my hands of any guilt and blame. I am but a messenger of the spirits. Your contract is with them, not me. You have entered this agreement of your own free will and so shall it be. There is no turning back now. Give me your hand.'

With a swift flicker, Ogbunigwe pierced the skin of my thumb with a blade, drawing the blood in a thick spurt. I saw the red drops hit the floor of his shrine with a hiss that had me almost bolting from the room. From nowhere, smoke suddenly filled the room, as if a thick fog had descended from the skies. The smell of blood was overpowering. My head was swimming, my eyes watering. My breath come out in short gasps. I saw movements in the fog, quick darting motions of figures I could not decipher. They seemed human, pale and ghastly, yet, too insubstantial to the sight. And surely, no human could move with such speed, even faster than hurricane. *What on Amadioha's earth were they?*

Ogbunigwe gave me a list of items I needed to bring to him for the preparation of the charms. When I heard the list, my blood almost froze in my veins. They included the hair from my dead child's skull, our husband's under-garment, a vial of my menstrual blood, the blood from a week-old baby boy and several other animal and human parts and herbs too numerous to recount. He also wanted hair from Nwanna's head – Nwanna, our husband's new son.

I felt my resolve falter at that last item. Why Nwanna's hair? Why not hair from any other child? I voiced my thoughts, but the great medicine-man hushed my words with a glare that put the terror in my heart. I wanted to flee from the skull-littered shrine, to hide away from the terrible visage of the witchdoctor. But I recalled his words, *"There is no turning back now."* I also remembered the melancholy face of my son, Ebuka and the arrogant swagger of Enu. I knew then what I had to do.

'It shall be done, Great One,' I bowed my head again, stooping to kiss the ringed toes of Ogbunigwe's bare feet. 'It shall be done.'

***

Ogbunigwe's list was daunting and almost impossible to secure. But as our people say, *there is nothing the eyes will see that will cause them to shed blood-tears*. A desperate need will always find a miracle. My will to bring back my son was as strong as an elephant's charge. I found my miracle in my wonderful sister, Gono, who had gone ahead to become a successful headteacher at a top secondary school, one of the handful of female head-teachers from our country, rubbing shoulders with the white Irish nuns who ran our education institutions.

As my father had long dreaded, Gono had indeed refused to give him a befitting son-in-law and dowry, preferring to earn and keep her own money instead. She had become a very wealthy and respected woman who some people predicted would have a successful political career in the new political climate that had won us our independence from the Queen of England. Men were now seeing the hidden beauty in my sister which our father had failed to recognise on account of her dark skin. With her striking ebony features and elegant carriage, my sister could have married the greatest prince in the world. But Gono had my wretched marriage as a constant reminder of what that vile institution harboured for women. She vowed never to relinquish her freedom and wealth to any man.

Gono gave me the exorbitant sum I requested for the purchase of most of the items demanded by the medicine man, Ogbunigwe. She neither asked, nor did I volunteer the reason for my need. As always, she was happy in my happiness and I again thanked Our Virgin Mother for blessing me with such a loving sister, whose kindness I did not deserve, not with the kind of person I had now become, a sinful pagan with little remorse.

Afterwards, for several days and nights, I agonised over the terrifying trip I had to make to *Ajọ-ọfịa* to obtain a palmful of my dead child's hair. It was a trip which I had always lacked the courage to attempt, a journey I could not avoid, a visit that had been waiting to be made since the day they dumped my son's little body in the unhallowed grounds of *Ajọ-ọfia*. It was a trip now inevitable in order to bring my son back to life.

***

For three nights in a row, I attempted to cut the hair off Ebuka's head when he visited me. I used a small scissors to cut off a generous amount of his hair, which remained thick and lush despite the ravages of the grave. Yet, every morning when I awoke, the hair, just like my son, were gone, leaving me with nothing but the little red shoes that remained as new as the day I bought them.

My son told me that I must go to *Ajọ-ọfia* to get his hair. He said he would lead me to his grave. He told me that his grave was a shallow grave, barely an arm-length in depth, as was the way with all unhallowed
96

graves. Accursed corpses required no respect or protocol. I could easily dig open his grave with nothing more than my farming hoe. He said it was a job I could complete in the course of a single night.

Ebuka knew why I needed his hair and the knowledge made him happier than I'd ever seen since he returned to me. It was strange, the contradiction in his age and demeanour. In size, he had not aged a day beyond the three years he was when he died. Yet, his speech and reasoning were that of an *Ozo*, a wise and titled old peer of the clan. He calmly informed me that he would not come back to me until the day I became filled with the seeds of his reincarnation.

'But my son, how will you know when I get pregnant if you don't visit your poor *Mami*?' I asked, my eyes pleading, my voice cajoling.

'I will know, *Mami*,' was all he said. 'I will know.'

And I believed him.

And so it was that on a moonlit night of still air and sleepless insects, I made my stealthy journey to *Ajọ-ọfịa* accompanied only by my son and my farming hoe. I had agonised over embarking on that trip on a night when the moon hung round and low in the skies, knowing that Queen Ill-fortune was most alert on such a night. Yet, it would take an infusion of the hearts of a thousand warriors to get me to attempt that terrible journey under a black sky, without the bright light provided by the demon queen. I therefore steeled myself to brave the mischief of that fearsome deity of bad-luck.

I started off just after midnight. In no time, I soon developed the vision of the night bat and the agility of the forest monkey as the journey progressed. I engaged in lively conversation with my little son to rein in my terror. Ebuka was as surefooted as the bush antelope as he navigated through wild vines and erosion gullies, leading me further away from Ukari village and deeper into the forest. The night seemed to go on forever till, suddenly, without warning, I found myself in a desert-like landscape populated with nothing but giant anthills and uncountable mounds that housed the corpses of the damned.

Like a macabre farm, the grave-mounds grew soured crops of ghastly white masks. Each grave was fortified with the charms masks and potions in clay jars to chain in the evil dead within the confines of the bad bush. A foul smell pervaded the corpse-farm, an odour of badness and decay; a vile smell that I'd tried in vain to wash off from my son's body.

My heart froze. My speech ceased. My head began to swell and expand, and my breathing hung. All sounds stopped, vanished, as if cocked inside a sound-proof bottle. The noisy insects that had accompanied us through the night, the barking dogs, the hooting owls, all ceased their clamour. Even the very air seemed to succumb to the stillness of the desolate and chilling landscape. In the unnatural silence, I heard the thudding of my heart like the beating of the drums of the masquerade dancers. I heard the harshness of my breathing and the roaring in my ears.

Then I saw them...*oh Jesus, Mary Mother of God*...I saw them all, the soulless inhabitants of the accursed land, *Ajọ-ọfia,* the doomed outcasts of the gods and men, the unclean! Gathered in a silent, waiting crowd, hollowed eyes dripping blood as black as tar, each posed in the manner of their demise, they impaled me to the ground by their appalling visage.

A young mother with a rotten foetus dangling between her wide thighs; a large man with a suicidal rope tight against his impossibly-angled neck; an albino that glowed inhumanly white beneath the brightness of the moon, his body bloated and battered from the beating that caused his untimely demise; a tiny baby wailing and writhing on the ground, his wide mouth exposing a full set of upper teeth; identical twin boys with skin charred by the lightning strike that killed them – they were all the abominations of nature and the rejects of men.

And amongst them was my son, my beautiful, sweet Ebuka, standing silently in the midst of the other small spectres, each doomed for dying before their parents or being born with abominations such as a set of teeth, an extra finger, a single testicle. One second, Ebuka was by my side, his tiny hand gripped firmly in my right hand. Then in a blink, he was gone, gone without a sound, without me seeing his departure, only to appear amongst the ghoulish gathering of the damned, the cursed inhabitants of the unhallowed grounds of *Ajọ-ọfia*.

The sound of my hoe hitting the ground resonated like a thousand footsteps in the awful silence of the burial ground. It also released the voices of the apparitions, who started to howl in an unearthly cacophony that chilled the marrow in my bones. My voice joined their discordance, terror and panic cloaking my screams. Prayers spilled from my lips, babbles, the distinct sounds of supreme lunacy. Inside my head, Queen Ill-fortune shrieked in glee, her cackle as manic as my screams. Above us, the moon grew fatter and brighter, revealing the ghoulish figures in all their undead horror.

I tried to run, turned to flee, feeling the hot piss of terror flood my thighs. I stumbled against a mask…*no*…the mask rose against my feet as if flung by an invisible hand. Then all the other white masks joined the attack like a sea of skulls, hurling themselves against my face, battering my body and my head till I fell onto a soft grave, feeling the mud cover my face and fill my screaming mouth. It was the same mud that clung to my son, the vile grave-mud of the unhallowed ground I'd tried in vain to wash off my son.

My fall stilled the masks. They fell to the ground with muffled thumps. From the corner of my eyes, I saw them scuttle away, countless white masks, like the crabs on the beach of River Niger, each returning to the grave-mound they guarded, their hollowed eyes watchful, dark and terrifying. In the sudden stillness, I heard another sound, a noise like the roar of the winds.

And suddenly, they were everywhere, the ghosts of the damned, in front of me, behind me, at my right side and left side. And when the light of the moon dimmed above us, I glanced up to see the flying ones, *Amosu,* witch night-flyers who had carried on their nefarious art even to the grave. I felt their hands on me; cold hands, clammy hands, pus-wet hands, peeling hands, skeletal hands. Reeking bodies swamped me, seeking the warmth of my blood, the light of my humanity, my very soul.

I tried to push, to crawl to safety on hands and knees, to be free of the repulsive touch of the foul undead. But I was but a woman, a weak and foolish human who should have known better than to challenge the might of the queen of malignancy on her most potent night.

But desperation was never a person of caution or reason. Desperation would dare the gates of hell and the wrath of Queen Ill-fortune to fulfil its goals. Desperation gave me the voice to scream out my son's name, to call for his aid and his intercession. Desperation fuelled my garbled explanations, my pleas for their forgiveness, my supplications for their help in finding my son's grave amongst the hundreds of unmarked mounds that grew in that accursed farm of corpses.

Suddenly, I was free - free of hands, of bodies, of voices, of the pulsating hate that had engulfed me and left me cowering on the cold hard soil of *Ajọ-ọfia*. Once again, my son was by my side, his little hands filled with an impossible strength, raising me to my feet, his face a mask of sadness, *oh Jesu, pity my soul!* So very sad and old.

I wanted to die and lie with him in that bad bush for eternity. *How can any mother bear to see her child abandoned in such a desolate and terrible place? How could I ever sleep in the warmth of my room when my only child wandered in the dark wilderness of these cursed grounds? How could I walk amongst the living when I knew that my son walked amongst the damned, the restless and angry souls of the accursed?*

As if he read my thoughts, Ebuka pointed to a small grave barely the size of a yam-tuber mound in a flourishing farm. It was guarded by a repulsive white mask that resembled a leering goblin. I shuddered as my eyes encountered that accursed object, reluctant to bring my person within its malignant reach. My heart still quaked with the recent memory of the white masks' vicious attack on me.

My son motioned me to dig, his small hands holding up my discarded hoe. Once again, my resolve was re-ignited as I stumbled my way to the small mound and started to dig. Through that moonlit night, I dug till the sweat lay on my body like a bucketful of water, till my palms went raw and bloody, till my joints ached as one crushed by a palm-tree, till my eyes ceased to see anything but brown hard soil, till my breath rushed in staggered gasps through open mouth and nostrils clogged by snot and dirt.

Till.... till I finally struck the brittle bones of my poor, poor son, dumped in that terrible grave without the dignity of a coffin.

I began to howl.

I slumped on the dirt floor of the grave and wailed - keened - mourning my dead son all over again as if he had died anew. The pain was as raw as the day the evil viper, *Echieteka,* stole him from me. My heart burnt with anger and pain, fury at the callous way they had discarded my son's body and a hurting pain that threatened to steal what was left of my sanity.

I felt the presence of the ghosts, felt their compassion surround me as I tore the hair from my scalp, knocked my forehead on my hunched knees, beat the ground with clenched fists and bawled my pain into the cold dark grave of my son. I felt his little hands on my face, stroking my wet cheeks, his small cold body nestling against me, his thin arms around my neck. I held him close, so tight, I would have squeezed the life force from his body if there was any left to destroy.

'I'm so sorry, my son,' I choked between hard sobs. 'I'm so sorry. Forgive your poor *Mami*. Please forgive *Mami* for not protecting you, for letting them do this to you.'

'Don't cry, *Mami*,' his voice was muffled against my chest. 'Don't cry, please *Mami*. Look, my hair is still here, see?' Ebuka pointed to his tiny skeleton which indeed still harboured a long bush of lush, black hair. The familiar icy chill coated my skin once again with the tiny, hard dots of terror.

That was the day I realised that hair was immortal. And it finally made sense why Ogbunigwe had demanded that particular item. Only immortality could confer life. My son's immortal hair would reincarnate him back to life. Nwanna's living hair would link the bloodline, ensuring a successful reincarnation.

I did not need a pair of scissors. The hair left my son's skull in an easy clump, filling my hand with its kinky soft texture.

'You have to go now, *Mami,* before the sun rises or there will be no one to show you the way back to Ukari. We have to sleep when the morning dawns. Come, let me take you back now.'

I allowed my son to lead me out of that terrible place, my eyes filled with tears, my heart breaking with sorrow at the tragic plight of those pathetic souls that haunted the grounds of *Ajọ-ọfia*. I knew some of them were guilty of the crimes that had consigned them to the bad-bush. But most of them were innocent, like my son, like those poor teethed babies. Yet, all of them were equally damned for eternity. *But not my son, not my sweet innocent baby. By Amadioha and all the gods, I'll free him from that terrible curse and return him to the loving fold of his family.*

I now had the final and most precious item demanded by Ogbunigwe, the great witchdoctor. Ebuka's hair would be the final piece in the charms that would secure the affections of our husband once again and germinate my womb with my son's reincarnated foetus.

***

When the door of my bedroom swung open a couple of weeks later and Agu stepped into my room, I knew that Ogbunigwe had lived up to his reputation. Even before he began stripping off his clothes, I knew from Agu's face that he had not come to inflict violence on my body.

From the minute I covered my face with the foul-smelling oil given me by Ogbunigwe, I noticed a growing look of desire on Agu's face. And when he unexpectedly called me by the long-forgotten endearment, *"Nkem"*, I knew that he finally belonged to me, at least in body, if not soul. Already, a cup of palm-wine laced with the cloudy liquid the medicine man had given me to feed our husband stood by my bedside, a drink which also had to be spiked with the residue of his semen before he drank it.

Afterwards, when Agu had drunk the charmed wine and once again mounted me, I noticed a difference in his *Amu*. It looked and felt double its original size and remained solidly erect even after his release. I saw the look of baffled pleasure on Agu's face as he observed his enlarged and turgid organ. It was the look of a young boy discovering his first tuft of manly beard.

Over the following weeks, Agu continued to visit my room every night. His desire was insatiable, and my body soon grew weary of the incessant demands made on it, coupled with the fact that his visits were affecting my son's.

Ebuka had not paid me a single visit from that terrible night he led me to his grave to collect his hair from the skeletal husk that lay beneath the shallow grave at *Ajọ-ọfia. Holy Mary! Jesus our Saviour!* I still shudder, still wake up in sweats, still glance behind me in unspeakable terror at the memory of that dreadful night.

***

As the weeks turned into months, Agu's nightly visits gradually increased to afternoon and evening visits. The intimate name, *Nkem,* never left his lips when he addressed me, even in front of strangers. Soon, malicious tongues began to wag, fuelled by Enu's spite. The words "Witch" and "Mamiwata" cropped up once again in reference to me. They were tags I hadn't heard since my son's death gave birth to new names, "*Akula*", mad-woman.

But this time, their insults left me cold. Despite the element of truth in their accusations, I felt none of the guilt and shame I'd felt in the days I was falsely accused. *What did I care about their feelings as long as I brought back my son to life?* The Holy Virgin knew I was paying my own heavy price, enduring the rough and incessant sexual attentions of our husband to achieve my goal. My secret place was raw from the persistent demands made on it by our husband and my soul was weary to its core.

And yet, despite the passing months and the increased frequency of Agu's carnal visits, my belly refused to germinate with the seeds of fertility. Nothing grew inside my soured womb. But something began to grow on our husband.

Chapter Ten

The first mole appeared on Agu's *Amu* on a Sunday afternoon. I know the precise time and date because I remember being dragged into my room as soon as I returned from Sunday Mass and mounted in rushed frenzy before I could even undo my *Enigogoro* head-scarf. I also remember feeling soiled and defiled by the act, considering I had just been sanctified by the Holy Communion taken from Father O'Keefe's righteous hands.

After the act was over, I noticed Agu starring at his *Amu,* which as always, jutted up towards the low ceiling of my room, bloated with useless seeds that could not fertilize my womb. I instantly noticed the spot on his organ, a spot more like a giant mole than anything else I could imagine. It formed a solid round mass at the tip of his *Amu,* its reddish hue contrasting starkly with the blackness of that organ.

Chickenpox! That was my first thought; *Agu has chickenpox!* Trust the wretched man to do everything differently. Other people got the pox on their faces but not Agu. Oh no! He had to go get it on his blighted *Amu.* By the next day, four more moles appeared and within a week, the entire length of his *Amu* was covered with the unsightly red moles.

It was about this time that I noticed a difference in his possession of me. It felt as if he performed the act for reasons other than desire, as if something else was driving his frenzied thrusts, an itch perhaps, an uncontrollable urge to scratch, relieve the irritation in his skin. But why use me? Why wouldn't he keep away from me till his pox or whatever it was ailing his organ was cured?

Because of Ogbunigwe's charms, you fool! The mocking voice in my head was as nasty as Queen Ill-fortune's cackles. I'd asked for our husband to be enslaved by desire and I had my wish. Something else told me those wretched charmed drinks I had fed him over the course of several weeks were equally responsible for the disgusting moles that were fast turning his *Amu* into a twisted grotesque appendage.

Conjugal exercises had never been pleasant with our husband, even at the best of times. Now, they were just awful, terrible acts of torture that tore up the tender skin of my circumcised womanhood and left me dreading the simple act of weeing or washing. My days were now lived in terror of those hurried footsteps headed to my room, knowing that my objections would be quashed by violent hands and thrusting hips.

I was raw and bleeding both inside and out, but our husband was oblivious to my pain. All he knew was the driving desire that kept him chained to my bedside. Agu would not discuss the state of his *Amu* with me. In fact, he seemed determined to ignore the ghastly thing, despite the fact that other alien bits had joined the moles, long spiky hairs and worm-like welts.

I tried not to look at that monstrosity. Jesus knows just how much I tried to keep my eyes away from it. But the eye is the master of curiosity. It will look where it should not and seek where it is forbidden. So, my eyes followed the gradual distortion of that organ, observing the festering malignancy of that benighted appendage as crusted pus was replaced by fresh eruptions and I wished…. *dear Lord*…how I wished I could sever that evil with a sharp knife and free us both from our nightmare.

We were now the talk of the whole village. Agu no longer stepped out of the house, seeing as he could not wear anything save the loose wrapper he kept secured around his waist. His visit to his *Dibia* had not cured his ailment, neither had all the ointments and antibiotics prescribed by the doctors at Park Lane Hospital.

I had tried to get an antidote from Ogbunigwe, something to cure our husband's organ and free me from the pain inflicted by that awful weapon. But the powerful medicine man had been like a stranger to me, aloof, cold. He reminded me that I'd made the choice of my own free will. The consequences were therefore mine to bear. He could not help me.

So, I remained a prisoner in my room, unable to walk without bowed thighs, writhing in agony from the lacerations inflicted by that punishing weapon. I had become the cursed jailor, suffering the same fate as my hexed spouse. Enu and the three fat sisters shouted to all who would listen that I had chained our husband with witchcraft, that he had lost his mind as I had lost mine. His business was failing, and his workers were running lawless. Enu was pregnant with yet another child and our husband ignored that fact and provided little for her comfort.

The news of Enu's pregnancy almost drove me wild with jealousy. Why should she have all the luck, a living son and another easy pregnancy, when I had been going through months of torture to achieve the same fate without success? Clearly, the blasted woman was born under a very good *Chi* despite her meanness.

Except she wasn't after all.

On a dark, rainy night, Nwanna got the runs. All night, I heard the sound of the housemaids rushing up and down the stairs as they emptied the child's potty. My room was still at the servants' quarters, so I could easily keep tabs on their comings and goings. Our husband had wanted to return me to my old room which Enu occupied, but I didn't want to leave the room that was my only link to my son. Ebuka must never come and not find me in my little room at the end of the servants' corridor.

Enu burst into my room a couple of hours later, rousing our husband from his deep sleep in my bed.

'Your son is dying, and you lie here like an idiot,' she shouted at Agu. Her eyes were red and puffy, her hair dishevelled.

'What's wrong with Nwanna? Can I help?' I asked. I felt a sudden pity for the woman. Despite everything, she was still a mother, experiencing a mother's hurt at her child's suffering.

'Keep away from my child, you witch,' Enu snarled, dousing my goodwill with her spite. I shrugged and turned away, feigning disinterest. Agu dragged himself up from my bed, waving Enu away.

'I'll be with you soon,' he said. 'Send for the driver to take him to Park Lane hospital.'

Enu stalked out of my room, slamming the door behind her.

'Nkem, I'll be back soon, ok?' Agu said, looking apologetic and guilty at the same time, as if he were committing a crime by attending to his sick son instead of spending time with me. *Ogbunigwe's charms had really done the works on him*, I thought with regret as I watched him hobble out of my room. I had not spiked his drinks in months, yet his *Amu* refused to heal and his slavish devotion to me refused to wan. *If only I could convert that attachment to a pregnancy…*

***

Nwanna died that same night. Even the white doctors at Park Lane hospital could not perform their usual miracles. They said it was cholera, the deadly sickness of the intestines. Enu said it was witchcraft. I had finally killed her son with evil juju, as I had long intended since his birth. The accusation chilled my bones, filling my heart with terror. *Oh Holy Mary! Don't let Nwanna's death have anything to do with my visit to Ogbunigwe and that tiny quantity of hair I'd taken from Nwanna's comb!*

For several days following Nwanna's death I paced around my room, enduring sleepless night after sleepless night. *How could I live with myself if I had a*

120

hand in that innocent child's death? How could I possibly forgive myself if I had been instrumental in sending that poor child to join my son at Ajọ-ọfia, the dreadful corpse-farm of the doomed?

I derived no pleasure at the thought that Enu's child now shared the same fate as my son, having died of a deadly disease before his parents. *What mother would wish the same torture on a fellow mother? Who could bear the thought of another innocent child confined to that tragic, desolate, and unhallowed ground?*

Enu's incessant wails and howls gave me no peace, just as my troubled thoughts gave me no sleep. Nwanna's hair I'd stolen was only supposed to re-ignite my son's hair, give it the living spark it needed to bring Ebuka back and link him to his father's bloodline, enabling his speedy reincarnation. The charm was not supposed to harm the child in any way. The harm had already been done to our husband; that guilt I freely acknowledged to myself. I could live with the damage done to our husband as I was sharing the agonising effects of it. Agu was no innocent or saint and I still remembered the horrors he'd put me through before Ogbunigwe's charms mellowed him.

But Nwanna was a different story. Nwanna was an innocent child. Soon, I found my way to Ogbunigwe's hut for the final time. From the resigned look in the witchdoctor's eyes when he saw me, I knew he had been expecting me.

'Nothing was supposed to happen to the child,' I screamed at him, tears pouring down my cheeks. 'You told me his hair was only needed to link my son's return to his bloodline.'

'Foolish woman!' His voice was scornful, albeit I detected a hint of compassion in his bloodshot eyes. 'I did warn you, didn't I? I am only a mouthpiece to the oracle and the gods never lie, not in my lifetime, nor in the lifetimes of my grandfather and great grandfather. I come from a long line of shrine-keepers and our juju have never failed.'

'Then why am I not pregnant? Why has my son not returned to me yet?' My voice was shrill in the dead silence of the night.

'A life for a life, a son for a son. Fear not; the bloodline is not broken. The oracle never lies. Return to your home, woman, and disturb me no more. My patience with you now wears thin.'

The witchdoctor waved me away with a casual flick of his hand, as if I were no more than a troublesome gnat, as if he hadn't just destroyed my life with his words, as if the death of an innocent child by his actions was no more than a splash of water on a Sunday gown.

I stumbled out of his hut and into the warm blackness of the night. My body was shivering uncontrollably. My heart was pounding painfully, and a loud voice kept screaming, *no! no! no!* inside my head. *What have I done? Oh dear Jesus, what have I done?*

***

Following Nwanna's death, Enu and the three fat sisters called several meetings of the clan to air their suspicions and vent their rage. The clansmen consulted several witchdoctors, who all pointed their fingers at me. They said that the curse of Queen Ill-fortune had been brought upon the family by my actions when my son died. They claimed that I had an unholy union with some powerful deities which defied their own powers. The house of Agu, son of Onori, was a doomed one. The only way to break the curse was to sever my link to the family.

The elders reached a decision that I was to be sent back to my father's house without delay. I read the fear and repulsion in their averted eyes as they told me my fate. Even the one I secretly called Grey-Hyena, the grey-haired clansman that had accompanied Agu that very first time they came to my father's house to seek my hand in marriage, would not meet my eyes. He spat on my face as he cursed me and called me a witch.

The only eyes that held no fear were Enu's. If hatred alone could kill, I would have been struck dead in seconds. Her eyes were the only gaze I could not hold in that large gathering of clansmen and clanswomen.

Our husband vetoed their ruling, telling them in no uncertain terms that I was his wife of no regrets, as he put it. He said that if anyone was to leave his house, it was Enu, not I. I heard Enu's sudden gasp, echoed by the rest of the family at Agu's words. His unusual stance confirmed all their suspicions but there was little they could do but wait, scheme, bide their time.

Until the day Agu finally succumbed to the infection that had journeyed from his deformed *Amu* to his veins, poisoning his blood and stealing his breath. He died in my bedroom, right on my bed, still trying to mount me even as death pulled him to its terrible door. The last words I heard from his lips were *"Nkem",* repeated over and over till his speech was silenced by eternity.

And I suddenly found myself at the mercy of all the enemies I had made in that accursed village, Ukari, helpless, childless and with no-one to protect me from their collective hate. I had no one to speak for me, plead my cause and spare me from the nightmare of my ordeal in the accursed forest of Ukari and the terrifying judgement of *The Tree of Truth.*

Chapter Eleven

(Ukari Forest – 5:15am)

Above me, heaven suddenly opens its mouth and spews down a thunderstorm on mankind. God's eyes flash His wrath across the skies and His anger roars over the world. In seconds, I am drenched, the rain washing the matted filth and blood from my body. I raise my face to the skies. My mouth is open as I drink in God's holy water of my salvation; real water at last, not the corpse water I've endured for days. The water rejuvenates me. It also rejuvenates the world of the living - and of the dead.

I see them. Suddenly, I see them in the deep gloom of the forest. They are everywhere; soulless spectres, the restless spirits of all the victims of The Tree of Truth. They crowd around the tree, howling, pleading their case, begging forgiveness for past crimes,

127

cursing, laughing – the pitiful laughter of the insane.
They fly against the tree, through the tree, around the
tree. They're drawn to the tree like moth to flame,
powerless to leave the scene of their demise or the
towering judge that sentenced them to sleepless
eternity.

I recognise some of their faces; Ugomma the
witch, Adaku the husband poisoner, one-eyed Chiadi,
the child-napper and Ijeoma the night-flyer. The great
tree had judged them all guilty, just as it might yet find
me guilty. It seems to have a peculiar penchant for the
evil souls of women. I do not want to be judged by The
Tree of Truth. I fear I may not survive its wrath. I pray
I do not become an unclean. Ajọ-ọfia *is no place for*
eternal rest.

I see my son, Ebuka, hovering beyond the ring of
salt. He is murky, coated in dirt and a strange darkness
that renders him almost indistinct. My heart swells with
delight then shrivels with terror at the look in his eyes.

They blaze with hate, with rejection. He points at me, an accusing finger and I hear his voice, louder than the thunder that had heralded the storm.

'You lied to me,' he screams. 'You lied! You cannot bring me back because I don't belong to Agu's Obi, his ancestral compound. His blood does not flow in my veins so I can never be reborn to his bloodline. I can never return anywhere. Only Nwanna can go back. His bloodline is intact. His mother is pregnant. You have doomed me to Ajọ-ọfia *for eternity. I hate you, Mami, I hate you,' his voice is terrible, a death-knell in my soul.*

I am wailing as I see my son fade into the night, the night that has suddenly turned as bright as day, lit up by the engorged moon and the spite of my unrelenting persecutor, Queen Ill-Fortune.

Then, I see Nwanna. He flies like all the other spectres, hovering in the clearing, laughing, his voice tingling like little bells, his child's eyes bright, happy and innocent. They bear me no malice, no hatred for my deeds. He glows with a dazzling brightness that is almost blinding in its intensity. Then he winks out, just like a star. And I am all alone with my guilt and my shame. The rain pounds down on me, relentless, merciless.

It has all been for nothing...nothing. After everything, all my suffering, all my hopes, my plans, everything. In the end, it has all been for nothing. If only I had gone back to Pastor Brother Ezekiel rather than that accursed witchdoctor, Ogbunigwe. If only I'd been born under a brighter Chi.

I hear a rustle. My head swivels. I see the waifs melt into The Tree of Truth, disappear into the massive trunk. The bark turns a sickly grey colour and the roots begin to heave. Oh Holy Mary! The Tree is alive! It moves! My head expands and contracts, my body a quaking mass. I know I am about to faint and sink into *dark oblivion. But I'm denied that escape, the evil being that I have become.*

My husband's corpse stirs, sluggishly, blindly, its arms lifting, slowly. A bloated hand gropes its way to its Amu. It clasps the erect vileness and starts to yank in a grotesque act of masturbation. I gag, my stomach heaving, my muscles contracting, aching, hurting.

The head turns, silently, heavily, towards me, where I cower at the edge of the salt ring. I begin to shudder. My entire body is one continuous rattle, my teeth, my bones. Oh Holy Mary, sweet mother of God, don't let him open his eyes, please... keep his eyes shut...

The lids lift and I see those eyes - bloody, yet black. They stare at me, fix me with their dead glare. I shut my eyes and cover my head with my arms. The heavens continue to pour, and I hear my moans, whimpers that sound like Agu's dog when it is whipped for misbehaving. I hear another sound, a croak, like a strangled man's dying gurgle. Then I hear the words, repeated over and over and over and over...

'Nkem...Nkem...Nkem...'

I jump to my feet and scream. I remember too late the salt ring, the charmed circle made by the powerful witchdoctors to keep me trapped under The Tree of Truth, and I hit an invisible wall.

Bright lights explode inside my head as I stumble back, falling, falling, right atop the rotten carcass of my randy husband. I feel arms encircle me, strong arms, skin slimy against mine, sleeked by decay and death.

The stench is overpowering and just as in my nightmare, I feel the hard thrust of that rotting, jutting deformity against my thighs, feel the touch of those putrid hands pushing, prising my thighs apart with a strength not of the living. The pain is excruciating, unbearable. I hear that awful gurgling sound repeat the accursed name, "Nkem" into my ears. My soul is pulled, dragged from my being by a malignant force beyond the realm of the living.

And I am screaming, shrieking. Queen Ill-fortune is cackling, crowing with unholy glee. The fat moon smiles down benignly at my unholy ravishment and impending death. God is thundering, roaring, helpless as He's always been in the face of mankind's tragedy. Our husband is grunting, panting. The spectres gather closer, their ashen faces greedy for my dying soul, eager to welcome me into their foul and restless fold.

From a distance, I hear the sound of the approaching villagers, murder in their voices. A small smile twists my bruised lips. They will be too late. I can already sense my soul fleeing, fighting for release from my dying body. I am happy to give it its freedom. I am ready to be judged, to end this accursed cycle and heaven willing, begin a better one. If nothing else, I shall share the same unhallowed grounds with my son and be with him for as long as the gods wish. It is a better fate than one of eternal sexual servitude to our husband, who is still panting his pleasure on my immobile, dying body. I feel nothing now, not the rain, not the pain, not even the fear.

I cast my dimming eyes at The Tree of Truth, awaiting its final judgement. But The Tree of Truth… The Tree of Truth is silent. And in its silence, I hear my judgement, my salvation. Gono's voice, my sister's raging voice rising above the din of the villagers, ordering the police to arrest my abusers, handcuff the lot. My heart soars, my tears flow. I feel arms around me, different arms, warmer, firmer arms, loving arms, human arms.

'It's okay; it's alright, my sister. You're safe now, do you hear? You're safe. You're coming home with me, okay? Can you hear me?' Gono's voice is urgent in my ears, her voice trembled by fury and pain.

I hear her. I also hear them; their unholy shrieks, their angry howls as they retreat into The Tree of

Truth, disappear into the approaching dawn, The Unclean, the accursed ghouls.

My heart soars. They will not have my soul after all, not this time... not yet. My blood will not fertilize the roots of The Great Tree; my soul will not be chained in eternal enslavement to my husband. The Tree of Truth has rendered its judgement and has deemed me worthy in the end. I am free…free…free…

Tears pour down my face as I look up to the greying skies. The moon is a fading round shadow, weak, powerless. I listen for that cackle, that terrible screech of doom. But for the first time in a very long time, I hear nothing. Queen Ill-Fortune is finally still, as silent as The Tree of Truth.

Ω

The Unclean

The Unclean

The Unclean

www.ingramcontent.com/pod-product-compliance
Lightning Source LLC
Chambersburg PA
CBHW022025170626
46808CB00003B/1061

9 7 8 1 9 0 9 4 8 4 3 7 5